KT-217-538

For my sister, Sylvia

A Beaver Book

Published by Arrow Books Limited

62-5 Chandos Place, London WC2N 4NW

An imprint of Century Hutchinson Ltd

London Melbourne Sydney Auckland

Johannesburg and agencies throughout the world

First published in 1988 by Andersen Press

Beaver edition 1989

© 1988 by Ruth Brown

This book is sold subject to the condition that
it shall not, by way of trade or otherwise, be lent,
resold, hired out, or otherwise circulated without the
publisher's prior consent in any form of binding or cover
other than that in which it is published and without a
similar condition including this condition being imposed
on the subsequent purchaser.

Colour separated by Photolitho AG Offsetreproduktionem, Gossau, Zürich, Switzerland.

Printed and bound in Italy by Grafiche AZ, Verona.

ISBN 0 09 962160 6

Ladybird, Ladybird
Ruth Brown

Beaver Books

Ladybird, Ladybird, fly away home,
Your house is on fire, your children are gone.

Ladybird, Ladybird, blown by the breeze,
Over the cornfields, and over the trees.

Ladybird, Ladybird, lands in some smoke.
There's really a fire; it wasn't a joke.

Ladybird, Ladybird, fly away, fly.
That frog has a hungry look in his eye.

Ladybird, Ladybird, which way to go?
The old snail is friendly, but he doesn't know.

Ladybird, Ladybird, please do not pause
Close to those dangerous, razor-sharp claws.

Ladybird, Ladybird, pass the pig by.
He's too full to think: too lazy to try.

Ladybird, Ladybird, go to the crow.
Ask him the way home, he'll probably know.

Ladybird, Ladybird, lost in the wood.
Squirrel can't help, though she wishes she could.

Ladybird, Ladybird, will she be blown
Further away from her children and home?

Ladybird, Ladybird, help is at hand.
The bees will show you the lie of the land.

Ladybird, Ladybird, all's clear at last.
Fly to your children, fly home to them fast.

Ladybird, Ladybird, safely back home.
It isn't on fire, and your children aren't gone.

They are all sound asleep, snug in their nest.
Now you can join them; at last you can rest.